THE SHOEMAKER'S GLASSES

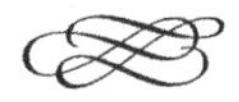

KYLE JOHNSON

Illustrated by

JOSH TUFTS

CONTENTS

1. The Shoemaker's Glasses 1
Reflections 9
2. Christmas Contest 11
Reflections 19
3. Penny Candy Christmas 21
Reflections 29
4. Christmas Angel 31
Reflections 39
5. Mischief Miracle 41
Reflections 49
6. Michael's Gift 51
Reflections 59
7. Silent Night 61
Reflections 69
8. A Christmas Prayer 71
Reflections 79
9. Follow Me 81
Reflections 89
10. Christmas for Santa 91
Reflections 101

THE SHOEMAKER'S GLASSES

Jonny Weaver turned his car into its usual parking space on Main Street, shut off the noisy engine, and waited. Within minutes another car pulled up alongside his.

He got out and stretched. Looking over the top of his car, Jonny greeted his lifelong friend. "Morning, Web."

"Morning to you, Jonny," Web said as he got out of his vehicle. "It's a cold one."

A light snow the previous night had made the town look like the cover of a Christmas catalog.

"Don't I know it!" With a gloved hand, Jonny patted the hood of his 1939 Woody Wagon. "I almost didn't get this old boy to turn over this morning."

Web chuckled. "Jonny, that car is older than you are. When are you going to get rid of that dinosaur?"

"Get rid of it? Are you kidding? It's a classic." He paused. "Kind of like me . . ." His voice trailed off with a hint of sadness.

Web frowned. "Are you all right?"

"Just feeling my age, I guess. My customers have no patience for a man who's slowing down. I can't seem to please them anymore."

"Now don't go getting down on yourself," Web said sternly. "You're the best cobbler who ever lived. Don't let anyone tell you differently."

Jonny gave a little nod of appreciation and then tossed a hand toward his friend. "Have a nice day, Web."

"Same to you, Jonny."

Web went inside his barbershop and Jonny walked two doors down the sidewalk in the other direction. When he reached Weaver's Shoe Repair, he raised his cane and rapped on the sign hanging from the eave. Powdery snow glistened in the morning sun as it floated to the ground.

Inside, he turned on the lights, hung his coat on a peg

beside the door, and flipped the OPEN sign in the front window toward the street. The start of another day.

A third-generation cobbler, Jonny had worked alongside his father and grandfather in the early days. Jonny learned quickly and it was clear early on that he had a gift. "Your skills are magical, Jonny," his father would say. Jonny could take a worn belt, bag, saddle, or pair of shoes and make them look like new again.

He peered at a picture of his father and grandfather hanging by the door. "Morning, Daddy, Granddaddy. I could sure use some of your wisdom. A cobbler's life has been good to me, but lately I've been struggling. I miss the old days. People are always in a hurry now. It's hard to convince them that quality takes time. And lately, with my sore hands and tired eyes, the work takes even longer. I wish people would be more understanding."

As he started to turn away, a movement caught his eye. Had his daddy winked at him? Surely his eyes were playing tricks. He put his nose up to the glass, looked from his father to his grandfather, and waited a full minute.

Just the imagination of a silly old man, he thought, walking away.

The familiar smell of leather and polish hung in the air as he surveyed his day's work. Items waiting for repair filled two shelves on the south wall. A shelf on the opposite wall contained items ready for pick up.

He'd barely settled in at his workbench when the chime above the door announced his first customer. A woman Jonny didn't know well walked in. Harriet Parker had dropped off her daughter's ballet slippers the day before and insisted they be ready that morning. He assumed the daughter needed them for the town's Christmas pageant. Unfortunately, he hadn't started on the slippers. He stood and walked to the service counter at the front of the shop.

Expecting her to be angry, he greeted her cautiously. "Good morning."

"I've come for my daughter's slippers," she said, in a voice bursting with grief. "What do I owe you?"

Jonny pursed his lips. He could tell she'd been crying. Now he really didn't want to deliver the news. "I'm sorry, Mrs. Parker," he said gently. "As I explained yesterday, I have several orders ahead of your slippers, and my policy has always been first come, first served."

He braced himself for fireworks. Instead, tears began to flow.

"You . . . you don't understand," Mrs. Parker managed to say, between sobs. I . . . I need them . . ."

Jonny's chest tightened. Feeling trapped, he breathed a heavy sigh. "Please don't cry. I'll put the slippers ahead of some other orders. They'll be ready by noon. But why the rush? The pageant's still a week away."

Mrs. Parker only sobbed harder and ran from the shop.

Jonny shook his head. *How could the woman be so impatient?* he thought, feeling himself bristle with irritation.

Minutes later, a woman with snow-white hair entered the shop. Against her bright red coat, her fluffy white curls stood out even more. Jonny was struck by the kindness in her eyes and the warmth in her smile.

"Good morning," he said, wiping his hands on a towel as he moved toward the counter. "May I help you?"

After looking him over carefully, she said, "I see I'm not a moment too soon. Goodness, Jonny, why are you so troubled?"

He raised his eyebrows. "I don't believe we've met, but you use my first name?"

"Using first names is a sign of friendship, Jonny. You may call me Martha," she said matter-of-factly.

Flustered, he cleared his throat. "Is there something you need?"

"Don't change the subject, Jonny. I've come to help. Now, tell me what's troubling you."

How could this woman he'd just met possibly help *him*? "It's nothing to fuss over. I won't burden you with my worries."

"Nonsense. That's why I'm here. Besides, we're friends now, and friends share each other's burdens. Tell me why you're so upset."

About to dismiss her query again, he caught a glimpse of something in her eyes that gave him pause. Though the sentiment defied all reason, Jonny somehow felt he could trust her. And he certainly needed a listening ear.

"Well, since you asked, I can't do as much as I used to do," he blurted. "By midday I have eyestrain and stiff hands. And my customers are so demanding. They want their repairs completed as soon as they place their orders. Instead of being grateful for the work, I cringe when I hear the door. I wish folks would be more considerate."

Martha nodded thoughtfully. "Jonny, how well do you know your customers?"

"What is there to know? They bring things for me to repair and I repair them. There's no mystery to it."

"I mean, how well do you know them personally? To understand why they're so impatient, it may help to put yourself in their shoes."

Was she serious? "That's all I do," he scoffed. "I know their shoes better than they do. I wish they'd put themselves in my shoes once in a while. That would be an eye-opener."

"This may be harder than I thought," Martha muttered, glancing away momentarily. She looked back at him. "Jonny, let me give you something for your eyes—to help you see more clearly." She fumbled around in her purse. "Ah, here they are," she said, producing a pair of wire-rimmed glasses.

Jonny frowned. "I can't take your glasses. How would you

get along without them? Besides, how could they possibly help me?"

"These glasses are special. Try them on."

To humor her, he put them on and adjusted the fit. He couldn't hide his shock when he realized she was right. "My goodness, I can see perfectly." Then he furrowed his brow. "But I can't take them. What if you need them?"

"They're a gift, Jonny. Anyway, I have several more pairs. But since you're uncertain, what if we were to make a trade? In exchange for the glasses, may I have some red shoelaces and a jar of black polish?"

"Take anything you like," he said, letting his gaze roam around the shop, enjoying the crystal-clear vision. "I'm overjoyed."

Martha selected a few items from a display case by the service counter and thanked him. As she went to leave, she suddenly turned around. "Oh, by the way, you should work on Harriet's slippers as soon as possible."

His eyebrows rose again. "How do you know about Mrs. Parker?"

"It's Harriet, Jonny. First names, remember?" She gave him a wink. "Now pick up those slippers and start mending."

Jonny huffed quietly. Who was she to tell him what to do? Then again, she *had* given him the best glasses he'd ever worn. He pulled the slippers from the shelf.

"Thank you, Jonny. You won't be sorry. You'll see." She put her thumb and middle finger together. "It'll be a snap."

There was a loud *crack* and Jonny lurched back in his chair as an image unfolded in front of him: A narrow road with hairpin turns. The sounds of screams, squealing brakes, and metal crashing against metal.

The scene faded and suddenly he was standing by Harriet Parker at the side of her daughter's casket.

Jonny tore the glasses from his face and groaned. What had Martha done? He should have known something dreadful had happened when he saw Mrs. Parker crying. If he'd only been more—

The realization stabbed him like a knife. That's what Martha was getting at.

He took deep breaths to calm himself. Then hoping to learn more of Harriet's story, he put the glasses on again. However, this time his eyes were drawn to Howard Kirby's work boots. Jonny saw a vision of Howard standing with a drooping head and shoulders in his employer's office with a pink slip in his hand.

When Jonny's gaze moved to a leather satchel that Hazel Rigby had brought in to him, he saw Mr. and Mrs. Rigby discussing a gift for their son, Brian, who was going off to college. They had little money, but Mr. Rigby had found a worn leather satchel in a trash bin and thought it could be repaired.

And so it went. Every pair of shoes and boots, every bag, belt, and saddle Jonny's gaze fell upon had a story—a story Jonny hadn't known.

Finally, after looking at every item in his shop needing repair, he slumped back in his seat. "I thought I knew my customers," he said sorrowfully.

Unaware of how much time had passed, he was startled when the door chime sounded. It was Harriet Parker. For a moment, he was mortified because the ballet slippers weren't ready. Then a wonderful idea came to him.

"Mrs. Parker—Harriet—please come in. I haven't repaired the slippers yet and I'm happy you're here to watch." He ushered her to a seat in front of his workbench. "These slippers must belong to a wonderful dancer. I can tell by the way the sole is worn." Jonny swallowed past the lump that had formed in his throat. "I know what happened to your daughter, Harriet. Is it all right if I call you Harriet? A friend taught me that using first names is a sign of friendship."

"Certainly," she said, as tears trickled down her cheeks.

Jonny cleared his throat and willed himself to stay composed. "Would you tell me about her while I work? She must have been extraordinary."

Harriet smiled softly. "I'd like that . . . Jonny."

For twenty minutes Harriet talked while Jonny listened and worked.

He replaced the leather outer soles, changed the draw-string, and mended the sash. With great care, he cleaned the slippers and made them look like new. Then he found pink tissue paper, neatly wrapped the slippers, and placed them in a special box, which he handed to his new friend.

"Harriet, I can't imagine what you're going through. Please accept my gift in memory of your dancing angel daughter."

At that, Harriet wept, and Jonny cried along with her. Eventually they wiped their eyes and Harriet prepared to leave. "What do I owe you?" she asked as she reached into her purse.

"Harriet, visiting with you has been a wonderful gift. And I have given you a gift in return. If you were to pay me, you'd be throwing my gift away."

She managed a little smile. "Thank you, Jonny. Your generosity . . . and friendship . . . will never be forgotten."

Jonny couldn't speak. He only nodded as she turned and left the shop. He walked to the window and watched her go, knowing something inside of him had changed. He was a new person thanks to the priceless gifts of two special friends. And he vowed that from then on, he would not only repair other's shoes, but also put himself in them.

REFLECTIONS

THE SHOEMAKER'S GLASSES

By definition, a shoemaker makes shoes and a cobbler repairs them. Regardless, when I was young, we used the term *shoemaker* when referring to the three local repair shops in our town. The shops were small and their floors and shelves were filled with pairs of repaired, or soon-to-be-repaired, shoes and boots. The air was heavy with the smell of leather and shoe polish.

People seemed thriftier and more resourceful back then. Maybe I remember it that way because I had very frugal parents. If something could be repaired or mended, there was no need to replace it. A pair of shoes or boots made at least one trip to the shoemaker (and sometimes several) before they were considered worn out. A new sole, a coat of polish, and a good buffing gave an old shoe new life.

While carving out the details of this story, I was captivated by the thought of someone who mends soles needing to have his soul mended. At times all of us get worn out and we may need a little soul repair. And, if we look around, we may find opportunities to help mend someone else's.

Christmas is a time for renewal. Like the shepherds and

wise men of long ago, we can look to the One who can repair every scuff mark, broken seam, and hole in our tired and worn souls.

CHRISTMAS CONTEST

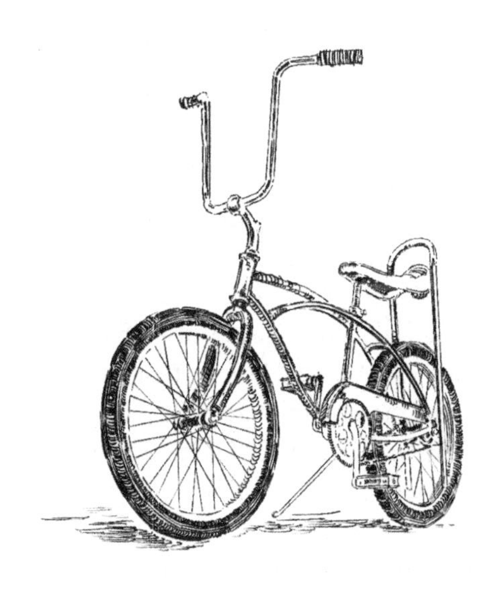

Hardy Pickett stomped hard on the pedals of his Schwinn Liberty. The back tire locked and the bicycle whipped sideways as it skidded to a screeching halt in front of Royal's Service Station. Something had caught Hardy's attention, and he wasn't going anywhere until he checked it out.

The station looked the same as it always had on the outside—four pumps with a canopy overhead, a garage with two bays, the Sinclair sign with its green trim and brontosaurus logo, and the red "Go with the Dino" slogan above the office window.

No, nothing about the outside of the station made Hardy slam on his brakes. It was something on the inside. Something in the window of Royal's office.

Hardy stared, mesmerized by the brand-new 1964 Sting-Ray bicycle with a banana seat and high-rise handlebars. The moment he'd seen a picture of it in the Schwinn catalog Hardy knew he had to have that bike.

He looked down sadly at his hand-me-down clunker. The old bicycle was heavy and hard to steer. Cankered with rust and pocked with dents and scratches, it was difficult for Hardy to imagine what it had looked like brand new.

His three older brothers had tried their best to put the bike out of its misery. His oldest brother had purposely left it behind his dad's work truck, hoping that when he backed out of the driveway the impact would be fatal. But his dad had straightened the frame and made it rideable again. His other brothers had been just as rough with it, but the Liberty was like a cowlick: it wouldn't stay down.

Hardy looked up again and fell into a trance as he admired the Sting-Ray. He imagined himself riding the coolest bike on the road through the streets of their little town. The spell was broken when he heard a voice.

"Looking to enter the contest for that bike, Hardy?" asked

the owner of the station, Roy Nance, as he walked out of the garage.

"Contest?" Hardy felt excitement surge through him. "What do you mean?"

"A coloring contest. See that poster in the corner of the window?" He pointed. "You must have been so busy gawking at that fancy bike that you totally missed it."

Hardy dropped the kickstand on his bike and ran over to the poster. As Hardy read, Roy explained the rules. "Starting Monday, kids in grades one through six can pick up an entry form, color the picture, and drop it into the box inside the office door. The contest will run for six weeks, and everyone is allowed one entry per week. Judging will take place Thanksgiving weekend. Winners will be notified the first week of December."

Hardy's jaw dropped. "Winners? You're giving away more than one bike?"

Roy gestured toward the back of the office. "See the other bike in that far corner?

Hardy pressed his face against the glass. "Yeah, I see it." Then he frowned. "That's a girl's bike!"

"That's right," said Roy with a chuckle. "A boys' bike and a girls' bike are the grand prizes. Smaller prizes will be awarded to the best boy and girl artist in each age group."

Hardy was so excited to tell his best friend, Duane, about the contest that he didn't wait for Roy to finish talking before he jumped on his bike and zoomed off.

Half a block from home, Hardy saw Duane sitting on his front porch. He was eager to tell Duane about the contest, but as he got closer, he could tell something was wrong. Duane's face was buried in his hands.

"Hey, Duane," Hardy called out cautiously. "What's up?"

Duane slowly raised his head. "Hi, Hardy."

"What's wrong?" asked Hardy. His friend sounded miserable. "Are you in trouble with your folks again?"

When Duane didn't answer, Hardy said, "You want to ride bikes? I have a dime. We could stop by IGA and get a Hershey's bar then go to the pond and skip rocks."

"That's the problem," Duane groaned. "My bike's busted. The front wheel is bent. When I hit a pothole, the wheel just folded because some of the spokes were so rusted. My dad says he doesn't have the money to fix it right now."

Hardy nodded knowingly. Duane's bike was in worse shape than his own. "Hey, I almost forgot," said Hardy, hoping his news would cheer Duane up. "I came to tell you that Royal's is having a coloring contest. The grand prize is a new bike. And not just any bike—a Sting-Ray!"

"Sting-Ray? Wow, that's neat! But a lot of good that'll do me. You're the best artist in the sixth grade. How am I supposed to compete with you?"

"You're a good artist, too," said Hardy. "Besides, Roy is giving away more than just bikes. There are other prizes for each age group." Hardy laid out the rules.

Duane brightened. "Well, I guess it couldn't hurt to enter. Especially if there's more than one prize. Say, if you can give me a ride on the back of your bike, let's head down to the pond."

THE FOLLOWING MONDAY—AND each Monday after that for the next six weeks—Hardy, Duane, and every other kid in town picked up a contest entry form. The picture they were to color showed a Sinclair station with a gas jockey washing a car windshield. A big brontosaurus was grinning in the background.

Hardy and Duane spent hours on each entry. Sometimes they'd compare their artwork. Hardy was skilled at shading and bringing a picture to life. With Hardy's encouragement,

Duane began to incorporate some of Hardy's style into his own entries.

"I can hardly wait for the winners to be announced," said Hardy one afternoon as the boys were playing in the park. "I think our pictures look great compared with some of the others I've seen."

Duane was instantly curious. "You've seen the entries of the other kids?"

"Some, not many. I was in the office at the station talking to Roy last week when Greg, Brent, and some of the other guys dropped their entries into the box."

"You'll win that bike, for sure, Hardy," Duane said. "It's my pictures I'm worried about. But thanks to you, mine turned out better than I expected. Hopefully I'll win the other prize."

On Thanksgiving Day, as Hardy sat down with his family for their annual feast, his father asked everyone to share something they were thankful for. When it was Hardy's turn, he said, "I'm thankful for the contest at Royal's, and that soon I'll be riding that new Sting-Ray."

"You sound a little too sure of yourself," his mother chided. "The winner hasn't been decided yet. Don't count your bicycles before the contest has ended."

Hardy waved his hand dismissively. "I'm not worried. I'm the best artist in the sixth grade. Even Duane says so."

"Didn't Duane enter the contest, too?" asked his father. "It seems to me he needs a new bicycle as much as you do. Maybe more."

"I told Duane I'd give him my old bike when I win the contest," he said smugly. "He doesn't have a bike right now, so any bike will be better than nothing."

The minute the words were out of his mouth, Hardy knew how shallow and self-important they sounded, and he caught the looks of disappointment his parents exchanged.

Throughout the meal, Hardy wanted to justify what he'd said. Wasn't he the best artist in the sixth grade? Wouldn't it be right if he won? But the longer his mind wrestled with those thoughts, the worse they sounded.

That night he had a fitful sleep. By the next morning, he felt so terrible he began to secretly hope Duane would win the contest.

THE FOLLOWING TUESDAY AFTERNOON, the phone rang. His mother answered, exchanged a few words with the caller, then motioned for Hardy to take the receiver.

Goosebumps prickled his skin. He could guess by her smile what the call was about.

"Hello?"

"Hardy, this is Roy Nance. I'm calling to congratulate you. One of your six entries was chosen as the best picture in our contest. We'd like you and your parents to come by the station Friday afternoon to claim your bicycle. The newspaper will be here to take a photo of you and the other winners."

Even though he'd been expecting this, Hardy felt the color drain from his face. He managed to offer a weak thank you before hanging up.

"That's exciting news, Hardy," his mother said. "A brand-new bicycle just in time for Christmas. You should be proud of yourself."

Hardy hung his head. He was anything but proud. "Mom, I need to run an errand. I'll be back in a while."

Before his mother could ask questions, Hardy was out the door and pedaling his bike up the street as fast as he could go.

When he got to the service station, Hardy found Roy in his office.

Surprise crossed the man's face. "Did you come to look at your new bike?"

"No, sir, but I've come to talk to you about that."

Roy frowned slightly and leaned back in his chair, gesturing for Hardy to take a seat on the other side of the desk. "What's on your mind, Hardy? You don't have the look of a boy who's just won a new bike."

"The bike's mine, right?" asked Hardy. "I can do whatever I want with it?"

"Of course, it's yours. You didn't think we were going to take it back, did you?"

"No, it's not that. But since I can do what I want with it, I want you to give it to someone else. I want you to call my friend Duane and tell him he won the contest."

"If that's what you really want, why don't you give it to him yourself after you pick it up on Friday?"

Hardy shook his head. "Duane can't know I won. You have to tell him he won or he won't accept it. This has to be our secret."

Roy's expression twisted into a look of puzzlement. "I thought you really wanted that bike? I saw the excitement in your eyes when you looked at it every time you came in."

"I found out there's something I want more. To be honest, I haven't had very good feelings about myself lately." He hung his head briefly then lifted his eyes to meet Roy's gaze. "I think this will help me get some of those good feeling back. Besides, Duane deserves that bike more than I do."

Roy smiled and nodded approvingly. "Sure, Hardy, if that's the way you want it, I'll call Duane tonight."

HARDY WALKED into his house just as the phone rang. Duane was so excited about the contest he went on for ten minutes. "That's terrific!" said Hardy. And he meant it. "I told you that you're a good artist. I can't wait for you to get your new bike."

When he hung up, he turned to see his mother standing behind him. Tears filled her eyes. "Roy called to tell me," she said, pulling him into a hug. "That was a noble thing to do. You gave me the best gift a mother could ever get."

Hardy looked up at her. "Mom, I'm sorry for the way I acted." He paused for an instant, then said, "You know, it's kind of a weird feeling. I can't explain it. I'm a little sad that I won't get the bike, but I'm really happy for Duane."

"That's the way it always is, Hardy. Real happiness comes from what you give, not what you get."

On Friday afternoon, Hardy stood in the crowd that had gathered outside of Royal's Service Station to watch the presentation. Duane's broad smile confirmed to Hardy that he'd done the right thing. He clapped loudly as Duane accepted his new bike.

When the ceremony was over, a girl from his class came up to him. "Guess you're not such a hotshot artist after all, are you, Hardy?" she said, nudging him playfully.

Overhearing the girl's remark, Roy gave Hardy a sly wink.

Hardy smiled as he glanced over at Duane, who was still talking with the man from the newspaper. "No, Polly, I'm not a hotshot. But with the help of some friends, I think I'm becoming the kind of artist I really want to be."

REFLECTIONS

CHRISTMAS CONTEST

When I was about ten years old, I entered a coloring contest sponsored by the local Sinclair service station. The picture we were to color was close to the one described in the story. I submitted five or six entries, but thought I had no chance of winning because one of my friends was a really good artist. I was shocked when I received a call telling me I'd won the grand prize—a new bicycle.

Though I was excited about winning, I was disappointed by the style of the bike I'd won. It was a traditional bulky Schwinn with a coaster brake and big tires and fenders—a clunky, boring bike. I don't remember voicing my displeasure, but I definitely felt deflated. I'd wanted a sporty new Sting-Ray with a banana seat and high-rise handlebars. The female winner actually did get a Sting-Ray, but apparently the bike I'd won was more expensive.

Looking back, I know I should have been more appreciative. I suppose most kids fall a little short in that category from time to time. Being a gracious winner can be just as tough as being a gracious loser. Over the years and after many life lessons, I've tried to become more thoughtful and considerate than my ten-year-old self.

Though I wish I'd learned to be more grateful and generous when I was young, a lesson learned is a valuable acquisition at any age.

Oh, and I eventually got a Sting-Ray, and it *was* pretty cool.

PENNY CANDY CHRISTMAS

As afternoon gave way to evening and the December sky turned dark, the Christmas lights of Downtown Coronet flashed on. The twinkling lights strung along Main Street led the way to a huge Christmas tree in front of City Hall. The brilliant display grew more extravagant every year in hopes of attracting holiday shoppers to the historic business district.

But Gabler's Five and Dime wasn't dressed for the holidays. There were no frosted windows nor any Christmas lights. There was no garland above the mirror behind the soda fountain; and, most surprising of all, there was no Christmas tree.

Milton Gabler loved Christmas trees. This year, though, the Christmas spirit was nowhere to be found inside the little store.

Instead, a sign out front announced: EVERYTHING HALF OFF. The cuts would eventually go deeper until everything was gone. In January, Gabler's would close forever.

Milt paused from sweeping. Leaning on the handle of his broom, he peered out the front windows. Smiling shoppers rushed by with their bags and boxes. Some of them used to be his steady customers. Nowadays most of them passed by on their way to somewhere else.

Things had begun to unravel after the big box stores came to town several years ago. Business had been on a downhill slope ever since, and the slope got steeper each year. After more than forty years of operation, this would be the store's last.

Milt sighed and gazed sadly around his store—his life's work. *So, this is it,* he thought. Would anyone care? He was sure that he and his little store would soon be forgotten

Gabler's was a remnant of a bygone era, a store with lots of variety but little supply. Milt reordered items only when a customer told him he was out of this or that. Folks didn't visit Gabler's to buy in bulk. They came for odds and ends: shoelaces, thumbtacks, screws, thread and sewing needles, soaps and lotions, a bottle of glue, furniture polish, or hundreds of other things.

More than a store, though, it was a place to gather—to wander the aisles and check out the knickknacks and doodads, or flip through the latest magazines. Swivel stools with worn vinyl seats stood up to a long counter in front of a soda fountain, where local seniors whiled away their mornings over coffee and donuts. The high school crowd showed up in the afternoon or early evening for sodas or milkshakes with friends. And they lingered because it felt good to be there.

Milt smiled as he thought about how the teenagers called him "Uncle Milt." It had started when his nephew, Joe, began coming into the store with friends. Joe naturally called him Uncle Milt, so a couple of his screwball buddies jokingly did the same. Pretty soon it caught on and every kid in town was calling him Uncle Milt. Now Joe's son, Joey, was working at Gabler's.

Where had the time gone?

Milt's heart ached as he walked down memory lane. He'd miss everything about the store, even those things that had seemed like an inconvenience at the time. Like Rose Taylor carrying on for twenty minutes about her rheumatism. Or Wendell Davies working himself into a lather over the price of gasoline. There were dozens more like them, but Milt endured it with patience because to him they were family and he knew they needed a listening ear.

"I finished breaking down the boxes and cleaning the bathroom, Uncle Milt. Is there anything else?"

Startled, Milt's breath caught and he jerked his head around. "Oh, it's you, Joey," he said, exhaling. "I must have gotten lost in thought. No, I think that'll be it for tonight."

"Is everything okay, Uncle Milt?" Joey hesitated briefly before saying, "I'm sorry about the store. I know it's hard to let it go."

"It's been a labor of love, Joey," he said, placing a hand on his great-nephew's shoulder. "It's like watching a part of me die. The saddest thing is that no one outside of our family will even notice. In some ways I feel like a failure." He swallowed. "Gabler's hasn't made much of a difference to anyone."

Joey frowned. "Don't say that, Uncle Milt. It's made a difference to lots of folks. It sure has made a difference to me and all the others who've worked and shopped here over the years."

Caught up in a rush of emotion, Milt couldn't respond to Joey's comment.

"What do you think you'll miss most, Uncle Milt?" Joey said softly.

This time, Milt didn't hesitate. "The thing I'll miss most is already gone. I miss the children—the ones who used to flock in here after school to buy a nickel or dime's worth of penny candy." He smiled dryly. "Of course, that was back when there was such a thing."

Inside a glass display case, Milt once kept dozens of small bins filled with Sixlets, Tootsie Rolls, Pixie Sticks, Smarties, candy necklaces, wax lips, Red Hots, Lemonheads, licorice sticks, Jawbreakers, and more. He missed visiting with the kids as they struggled to make up their minds. There were so many choices.

He'd found early on that he had more patience for their indecision if he chatted with them: *How's school? Who are your teachers? What subjects do you like? How are your grades? Does your father still work at the hospital? Don't you have a brother on the football team?*

Mostly it was small talk, but occasionally someone would volunteer comical or even heart-wrenching information. He remembered a young lady who lingered one day after the other kids had gone. She told him, through tears, that her parents were splitting up. A young man confided that his mother had cancer and it was sometimes tough to go home at night because he wondered if that night would be "the one." There were so many others over the years.

Milt didn't know whether he'd said the right things. He'd just tried to assure them that as bad as things seemed, happiness would come again. There was always hope for a brighter tomorrow. Milt knew something about hope being lost and then found again. When he and his wife, Maggie, lost their daughter, Elizabeth, when she was just three years old, he hadn't been able to imagine the darkness ever lifting. And when Maggie died suddenly a few years ago, the darkness had engulfed him again. But with the help of friends and family in both cases, his hope and happiness eventually returned.

JOEY SHRUGGED into his coat and said good night. As he headed home, he couldn't stop thinking about how forlorn his great-uncle had sounded. *There has to be some way I can help,* he thought, racking his brain as he trudged the five blocks through the snow. When he walked through the kitchen door, his serious look told his parents something was wrong. He just said he was tired and went straight to his room.

The thought still plagued him when he was in bed that night, causing him to toss and turn. He'd occasionally drift off only to awake with a start a few minutes later. Finally, at two o'clock in the morning, an idea came to him so forcefully that he got out of bed, grabbed a pen and pad, and jotted down some notes.

He knew it would take a lot of coordination, but it

seemed like the perfect Christmas gift for a man whose hope had begun slipping away. Finally, his mind relaxed and he slept peacefully until his alarm went off.

At breakfast, Joey's countenance was all lit up. "By the look on your face, I take it you've solved your problem," his mother said as Joey sat down at the kitchen table.

"Oh, yeah," his father said. "How about telling us why you were so glum last night?"

Joey was eager to tell his parents everything because he'd need their help. "You know how upset Uncle Milt is about his store closing. Well, last night he was really gloomy. He told me the thing he missed most was visiting with the kids who came into the store to buy penny candy. It might be a challenge," he said, looking at his parents, "but do you think you could find some of the kids from your day who have memories of buying penny candy at the store?"

Joey went on to explain his idea.

"Let's not just get folks from our day," his dad said, when Joey had finished, "but from the entire penny-candy era." His face beamed with excitement. "I'm sure we can get the rest of the family onboard. And with social media, I'll bet we can find dozens of people who want to help. My friends and I hung out at the store all the way through high school."

"There are only two weeks until Christmas," Joey's mom said, looking a little concerned. "Do you think we can really pull it off?"

"Uncle Milt needs to know that his life made a difference. We have to at least try," said Joey with a pleading look in his eyes. "Besides, it's Christmas—the season for miracles."

And with that, operation Penny Candy Christmas was born.

"We'll be closing as soon as we're finished with the chores," Milt said to Joey with a heavy sigh. He gazed out the store window with a deep sadness in his eyes. "The Saturday evening before Christmas and not a customer in sight," he muttered.

Joey nodded and tried to keep his face expressionless. Earlier in the day, he'd disconnected the bell that rung when someone entered the store. Thankfully, his uncle hadn't noticed.

At fifteen minutes to six, he called his uncle into the back room to look at a mess by the loading dock—a mess that he'd created as a diversion. "I don't know what happened, Uncle Milt. It must have been that dog that hangs out in the alley sometimes."

The plan was officially in motion. Joey could only hope everything would go smoothly and quickly out front.

Milt's jaw dropped at the sight before him as he emerged from the back room. He couldn't believe it. The room was filled with people clapping and cheering.

"Merry Christmas, Uncle Milt!"

Milt's eyes were drawn to a beautiful Christmas tree, strung with lights, sitting in front of the window where a Christmas tree had stood during the holidays for more than forty years. Large baskets filled with a variety of penny candy sat on the counter. Boxes of small red and green paper sacks, spools of Christmas ribbon, several pairs of scissors, and colored markers were next to the baskets of candy.

Milt's lips quivered and a tear trickled down his cheek. One by one, the throng of friends and family, whose lives he'd truly touched, came up to greet him.

"Thanks, Uncle Milt. Your talks kept me from hanging

out with the wrong crowd and making some real mistakes in my life."

"Thanks, Uncle Milt. You knew just what to say when my mother died."

"Thanks, Uncle Milt. I don't know how I would have gotten through those days when my father was away in the military without your encouragement."

Each person shared their story. Then they filled a sack with penny candy, cinched the top with ribbon, and wrote their name on it before hanging it on the tree.

Overwhelmed with emotion, Milt's tears now flowed.

AFTER SIXTY-NINE SACKS had been hung on the tree, the group gathered around it to sing Christmas carols. As "O Christmas Tree" floated softly through the store, Joey sat on a stool at the far end of the counter taking it all in.

His mother caught his eye and gave him a wink. He could only manage a slight nod back to her as he swallowed hard past the lump in his throat. Hope had been found. The little store that time forgot had made quite a difference after all.

Joey knew the memory of this night would stay with him forever. "Thanks, Uncle Milt," he whispered.

REFLECTIONS

PENNY CANDY CHRISTMAS

I have fond memories of the mom-and-pop shops in our little town that sold penny candy (when there was such a thing). In those days, if you had a nickel or dime, you were all set. With a sack full of Sixlets, Tootsie Rolls, Pixie Sticks, Smarties, licorice sticks or any of the other varieties of candy, you could ride your bicycle with friends to somewhere quiet and enjoy your sweet treasure. A memory of the owner of one of my favorite stores gave me the idea for Milt.

The older I get, the more I tend to reminisce. While working through the details of Uncle Milt's feeling gloomy and needing a lift, my thoughts went back to the cement irrigation ditch in front of my boyhood home. The ditch butted right up against the road. If people weren't aware of it when they came to visit, they'd sometimes drop their front tire into the ditch. Dad would send me or one of the other kids in our family to get a couple of cinderblocks. He'd then jack up the car until we could slip two blocks under the tire. With the tire at street level, the driver could turn the wheel and pull away safely.

From time to time, no matter our age, we all need someone to lift us up until we're able to pull out of our troubles. Keep the jack and cinderblocks handy.

CHRISTMAS ANGEL

It was a week before Christmas and Beth Reed braced herself against the cold as she walked swiftly from her car to the rear entrance of Mountain View Diner. The December wind howled, sending powdery snow swirling around her. Late, again, she hurried inside and pulled the door shut.

After punching her timecard, she shrugged out of her heavy coat, hung it on a nail by the door, then walked through the kitchen toward the dining area, careful to avoid the office. Just when she thought she'd made it without being noticed, a stern voice calling her name stopped her in her tracks.

She twisted her mouth into a guilty frown and slowly turned to face her boss. She didn't like getting lectured, but part of her was too tired to care.

"This is your third late in the past two weeks, Beth. You need to be on time—every day!"

"I know, Ken. I'll do better, I promise," came her standard response.

"See that you do." He returned to his office.

Exhaling, Beth closed her eyes and steeled herself for another agonizing shift, feeling more alone than ever.

An only child, she'd been heartbroken when her mother passed away after a long illness. A senior in high school at the time, Beth left for college shortly after graduation. Within two months, her father had found a new love. They married and moved out of state before Beth had completed her freshman year.

Beth grimaced as the memory assaulted her. *How could he even think about marriage so soon?* To her it was the ultimate betrayal and she hadn't spoken to him since.

Unable to concentrate on her studies, she dropped out of college and now lived by herself in a cramped one-bedroom apartment. Each day felt like a chore—just something to get through. And each night she'd lie in bed pondering her pathetic life and cry herself to sleep.

She'd been working at the diner for two years. Though she'd never done that kind of job before, she hoped it would help her escape the constant loneliness. But in her grief, she found herself barely able to acknowledge the customers and her coworkers, paying them no attention beyond what the job required. As a result, others paid little attention to her—until John came into the diner.

Shortly after receiving the scolding from her boss, Beth was mechanically pouring coffee for two construction workers when the diner's front door swung open. A short, round man with white whiskers took a seat on one of the stools.

What an odd character, Beth thought, as she eyed his red-and-green checkered shirt, broad-waisted pants, and green suspenders. She peered at him curiously as she moved down the counter to take his order. Something about him looked familiar, but she couldn't place him.

Although his rosy cheeks and bright smile were engaging, she did her best to keep her emotional defenses up to avoid getting hurt again.

"What'll it be?" she said in a careless tone.

His kind but piercing eyes looked straight into hers. "First," he said, "I wish to see a smile."

Beth narrowed her eyes. "Mister, if I had something to smile about, I'd do it."

The man frowned. "Who has stolen your happiness?"

"Let's just focus on your order. What can I get you?"

"Since you're taking my order, I think it would be nice if we knew each other's names. I'm John. I see on your tag that your name is Beth."

"Now that introductions are out of the way," she said sarcastically, "what would you like?"

"All right, Beth, if that's the way you want it. I'll have orange juice, a short stack, and two eggs over-easy."

She placed John's order with the cook and returned with a glass of juice. Before she could leave, John said, "Beth, you seem awfully blue. Maybe it would help to talk. I'm a good listener."

Beth turned away, momentarily taken aback. It had been a long time since anyone had shown interest in her. *Still, you know nothing about this man,* she reminded herself. "Your breakfast will be right up. Let me know if you need anything in the meantime." She turned on her heel and walked off.

For the next thirty minutes, she avoided John except to deliver his food and refill his glass. The last thing she needed was more questions to potentially crack the walls she'd so carefully built around herself.

As John got up to leave, Beth watched him from a safe distance. He dropped money on the counter then scribbled something up on the back of his tab. When he'd gone, she picked up the tab and was surprised to see these words: *Faith, hope, charity, these three.*

Why did he leave this? she wondered. She recognized the reference as scripture but didn't have a Bible of her own.

She thought about the words all during her shift. After work her curiosity got the best of her and she dropped by the city library. She grew more confused when she read the full verse, from 1 Corinthians: "And now abideth faith, hope, charity, these three; but the greatest of these is charity."

She tried to brush it off, but the verse nagged at her thoughts. And that night, she had a dream. Two women were pacing on a street corner and looking down the road as though waiting for someone. One woman finally said to the other, "What could be keeping her? If she doesn't come, we'll never get to Beth."

Beth awoke with a start and was unable to go back to sleep.

When John came into the diner the next morning, Beth confronted him as soon as he sat down. "What did you mean by that note yesterday? I had the weirdest dream last night, and I think it had something to do with that verse."

"Do you want to talk or take my order?" asked John brusquely. "Yesterday you wanted nothing to do with me."

She felt a small pang of guilt. "Look, I'm sorry about yesterday," she said, softening a little. "I'll take your order, but then I want answers."

After placing John's order, she described her dream to him and asked again about the verse.

"That scripture was about the things you need," he said. "You must think so, too, to have had such a wonderful dream."

"Who said it was wonderful? I dreamed about two women on a street corner."

He chuckled. "Would you like me to explain?" he asked with a sly wink.

"Yes, tell me," she said, unable to keep the eagerness from her voice.

"I will, but first you have to do something for me. It's an easy thing, really. But it may take a day or two to see results. Are you willing?"

Skeptical, Beth frowned. "How easy is it? And why will it take two days?"

"All I want you to do, Beth, is smile and greet each of your customers pleasantly. Can you do that for the next two days?"

"Maybe I don't want to know after all." She walked away grumbling to herself. *Who does he think he is, asking me to change? Why should I?*

That night, Beth had the dream again. She awoke in a

sweat and tossed and turned the rest of the night thinking about John's request.

She was frazzled the next morning when John came in.

"Good morning, Beth," he said with a knowing smile. "You seem a little . . . peaked. I can tell you have some questions for me."

She looked at him sternly. "You know what's happening to me, don't you, John?"

"Happening?" he said wryly.

"Don't play games with me." Her eyes narrowed. "I serve your breakfast, remember?"

"All right," he said, holding up his hands in mock surrender. "Are you ready to do what I asked?"

She hesitated at first but finally agreed. If she wanted to know the meaning of her dreams, she had to take a chance. "But you have to promise to tell me everything after that."

He nodded. "See you on Friday. And, by the way, I'll know whether you held up your end of the bargain."

Her eyes filled with wonder as John left the diner. *How could he possibly know?* she thought. But, given all that had happened, she didn't doubt it was true.

Gathering up all her courage, Beth began greeting customers in the way John had instructed. After the first three or four times, her smile felt natural and her kindness wasn't forced. And her customers responded. Even those who'd been coming in for years treated her differently. They left bigger tips, and some told her to have a nice day as they were leaving. One man said, "It's so nice to come in out of the cold and see a warm smile. It makes my day."

Beth was stunned. All this time, she'd been wondering why no one had ever treated her with kindness. *I guess kindness is like a magnet,* she thought. She liked the idea that all the kindness one gave could attract an equal or greater amount of kindness.

After the second day, which had reaped equally impressive results, she lay awake in bed thinking about the change in her customers and the meaning of John's note. When she finally drifted off to sleep, she had another dream. This time she was in her apartment. She heard a knock at the door, and when she answered, the same two women from her previous dreams were standing outside, smiling from ear to ear. A third woman waved at them from inside a car parked out front.

Beth awoke and sat bolt upright. *Of course! These three. Faith, hope, charity*. How could she not have seen it earlier?

John greeted her cheerfully the next morning as he sat down at the counter. "Good morning, Beth. How was your night?"

Though Beth was physically tired, she couldn't remember the last time she'd felt so energized. She reported the results of the experiment. "But I didn't have to tell you, did I?" she said. "Somehow, you already knew. You probably also know I had another dream." She paused. "Who are you, John? Why did you come to me?"

He looked into her eyes. "I'm someone who cares about you very much, Beth. Many people care about you, and that's why I'm here."

She swallowed, trying to stop the tears from falling that had formed in her eyes.

"After your mother died," he continued, "you lost all faith and hope. Faith and Hope were the two women on that street corner. They were waiting for Charity to take them to you. When you did what I asked, you began to develop love—charity—for others. By the time you had the second dream, there was enough charity in your heart that you had begun to regain some faith and hope. Charity brought Faith and Hope to your door. Do you understand?"

She nodded. "Did you know my mother, John?" Beth said, her voice cracking. "Is that why you're here? I've been so bitter since Mom died. I thought no one loved me . . . and that God had forsaken me." A tear escaped and rolled down her cheek. "I gave up on God and everyone else."

"God has always been close by, Beth. And you have more people watching over you than you can imagine. Your mother hasn't forgotten you. But she wants you to move on —to love again."

Unable to contain herself any longer, Beth broke into a full sob. She bent down to get a tissue from under the counter, and when she rose again, he was gone.

That night, Beth pulled a scrapbook from her closet. Looking at the photos, she relived fond memories of her childhood, especially those with her sweet mother. Half an hour into her private family reunion, her gaze fixed itself on a black-and-white photo. She gasped. The image was faded and grainy, but there was no mistaking the face.

She took the photo out of its plastic cover and checked the back. There it was, confirmation in pale black ink: *Great Grandpa John.*

Tears rolled down her cheeks again, but this time they were tears of joy. She marveled that she was actually loved. And that her very own angel had come to let her know.

REFLECTIONS

CHRISTMAS ANGEL

When we have faith and hope we place ourselves on a higher plane. We have the spiritual wherewithal to care more fully and love more deeply. And reaching out to others through simple charitable acts, such as a smile or a kind word, can have a huge impact on our faith and hope. As Beth learned in this story, kindness is like a magnet. Kindness or love (charity) causes faith and hope to swell within us.

While the connection between faith, hope, and charity was the focus of "Christmas Angel," this story is also a reminder that there are angels among us. Heavenly angels might not pull up a stool next to us in our favorite diner, but that doesn't diminish their influence in our lives. Seen or unseen, heavenly helpers are just as real as the earthly ones we see doing angelic things every day.

God will not forget us. If we seek to draw upon the powers of heaven, for ourselves and for those we love, angels will always be nearby. In this, I have complete faith.

MISCHIEF MIRACLE

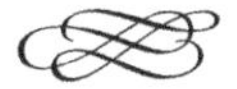

Ryan Brooks sat on a bench outside Harris Electronics while his dad dropped off a clock radio for repair. The unseasonably mild November weather had most folks in their shirtsleeves. He stretched his arms across the back of the bench and basked in the warmth of the of the afternoon sun.

"'Sup, bro?" The loud voice jolted Ryan out of his relaxing daydream. He looked over to see his buddy Steve Ross plop down casually beside him.

"Just waiting for my dad and catching some rays," he replied, trying to match Steve's degree of cool.

They traded small talk for a minute or two, mostly about girls, then Steve said in a hushed tone, "Hey, look. It's old Half-a-Deck."

Ryan glanced up to see a man in a long coat and tattered wide-brim hat shuffling down the sidewalk. Like Steve, Ryan only knew the man by the nickname everyone called him.

"Watch this," Steve said. As the class clown, he always had some gag device ready to whip out at a moment's notice. He stood up and extended his hand. "Put 'er there, pal."

The man grabbed the outstretched hand and was met by a shock from the buzzer Steve had hidden in his palm. He jumped back with a look of hurt in his eyes.

Ryan busted out laughing along with Steve, and the man turned and hurriedly hobbled off.

"What's going on?" Ryan's dad, Cliff, asked gruffly as he emerged from the store.

Ryan quickly stifled his laughter.

"Oh man," Steve said, giving his watch a bogus glance, "gotta run. See ya, Ryan." He took off.

"What did you do to Earl?"

"Earl?" Ryan said, avoiding his dad's intense stare. "You mean old Half-a-Deck? Just having some fun, that's all.

"What did you call him?" his dad growled through clenched teeth.

Ryan knew he was in a tight spot and he tried to find some wiggle room. "Hey, it's not just me," he argued. "Everyone calls him that." Then he smugly added, "You have to admit, the old guy isn't all there."

If looks could fry, Ryan would've been reduced to charcoal. He winced, knowing he'd struck a nerve. "Get in the car," his father ordered. "Now!"

Ryan huffed as he got into the car. His feelings vacillated between angry and worried as they drove. He knew he shouldn't have made that last comment to his dad, but he wasn't the one who caused all of this.

After traveling several blocks east, Ryan's dad stopped the car in front of the city newspaper office. The Clarion was a beehive of activity, mostly with folks who had personal items to sell or local businesses trying to get their specials in before the deadline.

"Let's go."

Ryan got out of the car without asking questions and followed his father. They skirted around the line at the classified counter and took the stairs down to the archives. A man with a pure white beard got up from his desk and came to the counter when he saw them walk in.

"Cliff. It's been a while. What can I do for you?"

"Hello, Skip. Do you have any football highlights from '68?"

Skip seemed to know exactly what Cliff was looking for. Behind him were rows of newspaper-sized filing cabinets. He walked down an aisle marked *1965–1970* and disappeared.

A few minutes later, he returned with a paper from October 1968. "Here's the last one. I can't let you have it, but you're welcome to look through it over there." He pointed to a big square table.

As he and his father sat down, Ryan finally broke the silence between them. "Dad, what are we doing here? What's this all about?"

His dad thumbed through the paper, found the piece he was looking for, and pushed it in front of Ryan.

All-American Earl Cooper rushed for three touchdowns and caught a pass out of the backfield for another score as the Mustangs crushed Riverside 42–10 in this battle of unbeatens. Riverside had no answer for Cooper, who rumbled for a career-high 326 yards.

"Earl?" Puzzled, Ryan looked up at his father. "Half-a-Deck?"

Cliff folded the paper and returned it to Skip. "Come on," he said, without looking at Ryan.

Ryan's thoughts were all jumbled as he and his father left the newspaper office. *How could the man Steve pranked on the street be the same one who set records on the football field?*

Cliff and Ryan resumed their silence as they drove out of town, heading west. Three miles out, the highway curved sharply. Cliff found a safe place to pull off just past the bend. He motioned to Ryan and they both got out.

"Do you know where we are?" Cliff asked.

"Of course, I do." Ryan pointed back toward the curve. "That's Cooper's—" The words caught in his throat as the realization hit him. "Bend," he finally managed to say.

"That's right," Cliff said coldly. "Cooper's Bend. It's named after Earl Cooper, the man you and your friends call Half-a-Deck. On October 25, 1968, the night of that record-setting performance you just read about, Earl was driving back to town after taking his girlfriend home. They'd been out celebrating the win. Unfortunately, someone else had been celebrating, too. A drunk driver drifted into Earl's lane. The driver of the other car died at the scene, and both of Earl's legs and one of his arms were badly broken." His voice softened. "Most devastating, though, was the brain trauma—the reason you and your friends call him that awful name."

Dumbstruck, Ryan could only stare out the window as they drove back toward town. When his dad turned onto Watson Avenue, Ryan knew the lesson wasn't over. A few blocks later they pulled up in front of a care center—a state facility.

Ryan took a deep breath. "Earl lives here, right?"

"That's right. Earl has lived here since his parents died. He's now a ward of the state. Let's go."

"Dad, we don't have to go in there. I've seen enough to know that what Steve and I did was wrong."

"Of course, you're going in," Cliff said with a sly smile. "How else will you be able to volunteer?"

Ryan went pale, and he felt as though he had a boulder on his back as he followed his father inside.

Cliff approached the front desk. "My son here wants to volunteer for two hours each Saturday for the next four weeks. How do we get the ball rolling?"

What! Ryan wanted to scream. His jaw dropped so far it nearly hit his chest. As they walked to the car, he argued, "Dad, I said I'm sorry. It was Steve's fault. Why are you doing this to me?"

"I'm not Steve's father, I'm yours. And it's my responsibility to teach you," said Cliff. "Someday I hope you'll understand."

They rode home without a word.

ON RYAN'S first Saturday at the care center, Thanksgiving weekend, a massive storm dumped six inches of snow on the ground. He spent the two hours shoveling walks, all the while cussing his dad. The weather had cleared by the following Saturday, and he was enlisted to wash windows. His third assignment was emptying trash cans and replacing the liners. Ryan's parents had instilled in him a sense of responsibility, so he tried to do a good job on each assignment. But he still resented his dad for making him be there in the first place. The punishment was completely unjust—after all, he'd only been a bystander.

On Ryan's fourth and final Saturday, one of the regular kitchen workers was sick, so Ryan was assigned to fill in. Clearing dishes and wiping tables wasn't his idea of a good time, but it beat shoveling snow.

When he noticed Earl take a seat across the room, Ryan knew what he had to do. *Maybe Earl won't remember that day downtown,* Ryan thought as he approached. *Or maybe he doesn't know I was there.* After all, it was Steve who'd pulled the prank. But when Earl caught sight of him, he stiffened and turned away.

Ryan's heart broke. *There must be some way to let Earl know how sorry I am,* he thought. As he agonized over the situation, an idea struck him like lightning and he knew exactly how he could make things right.

TWO DAYS BEFORE CHRISTMAS, the clouds gave way to a beautiful December day. Ryan went downtown hoping to find Earl. He scoured every street in the business district and had almost given up when he finally spotted him, sitting on a bench facing the Christmas display in the window of Martin's Department Store. His concentration never broke as he focused on one particular figure in the Nativity scene. His eyes gleamed with pure love as he worshiped Baby Jesus.

Though Ryan hated to interrupt the reverent scene, he stepped forward and said, "Hello, Mr. Cooper."

Earl tensed and wouldn't look in Ryan's direction.

Summoning all of his courage, Ryan cleared his throat. "Mr. Cooper, I'm sorry for what I did a few weeks ago. I hope you'll forgive me." He bent down and handed Earl a gift wrapped in bright Christmas paper. Earl's face lit up, and he raised his eyes to meet Ryan's.

"Merry Christmas," Ryan said. "Go ahead. Open it."

Earl tore away the paper to reveal a shiny new football. Across the front were the words *Earl Cooper, All-American 1968.* As Earl examined the gift, turning it over and over, a tear trickled down his cheek. Then he hugged the ball tightly, and his tears flowed.

Ryan sat next to Earl, wrapped an arm around his broad shoulders, and cried with him. And in that moment, a warm feeling washed over Ryan and he knew his gift had been accepted—and not only by Earl.

REFLECTIONS

MISCHIEF MIRACLE

One day when I was around fourteen, my dad and I were about to enter the local grocery store when Earl (not his real name) came up to us. Usually wearing a long coat and a battered hat, he was a fixture in our little town. On any given day, you were likely to find him walking the streets. Though older, because of an intellectual disability he was like a little child.

Earl was fascinated by Dad's hearing aids. Dad was legally deaf, but with the help of his powerful hearing aids, which were large and easily noticeable, he could hear some of the loudest sounds. Though he couldn't let Earl handle his hearing aids, Dad reached into his pocket, pulled out a shiny new hearing-aid battery, and handed it to him. Earl looked up at Dad and smiled. He looked at the battery and smiled again. Then he walked away admiring his new treasure.

A small thing, for sure, but it touched Earl's heart—and mine.

From time to time, we all need someone to give us a battery. It might be as simple as a friendly smile, an encouraging word, a listening ear, or a helping hand.

Give someone a battery this Christmas.

MICHAEL'S GIFT

Twelve-year-old Michael Barratt brought his bicycle to a screeching halt in front of his great-grandma's house. He stared in amazement. The cool autumn air had certainly done its duty. An inch of copper, orange, and yellow leaves blanketed Grandma Esther's lawn.

Since Grandpa Paul passed away, it had become Michael's job to take care of his great-grandma's yard. He didn't mind raking leaves, as long as he didn't have to do the whole yard at once. Besides, she always paid well. And every cent came in handy at Christmastime.

Michael's family lived only three doors down, so he and Grandma Esther had developed a tight bond over the years. He'd frequent her house, where they'd enjoy milk and cookies together and he'd help her out by doing small chores. His older sister, Hannah, cleaned Grandma Esther's house once a week, and his father took care of the big stuff: repairs and maintenance. Grandma Esther had always been there and Michael couldn't imagine life without her.

As Michael raked, he glanced through the front window from time to time wondering what he could get her for Christmas. The little money he earned from leaf raking wouldn't go far. A fancy gift was out of the question. Still, he wanted to give her something special.

That night, while his mother was fixing dinner, Michael scooted a stool up to the kitchen counter and continued mulling over what he could give Grandma Esther that would be unique.

"Is something on your mind?" his mother finally asked.

He glanced up at her. "What's something special I can get Grandma Esther for Christmas?"

"Hmm." His mother leaned on the countertop. "That *is* a good question. You know, she's in that time of her life when she really doesn't need another knickknack or kitchen gadget. The things that are important to her can't be bought in any store."

Michael frowned.

"Remember when we had that discussion about spiritual gifts?" his mother continued. "Well, I think you have several, but one that I especially admire is your ability to listen. When others are clamoring to have their voices heard, you seem to be able to take everything in and only speak when the time is right."

"I don't understand," he said, more confused than ever. "How will that help me find the right gift for Grandma Esther?"

"Listen. Visit with your great-grandma and listen for clues. But rather than listening with your ears, listen with your heart. If you do that, I'm sure that before Christmas you'll come up with the perfect gift."

Michael wasn't so sure, but he decided he'd take his mom's advice.

ON THANKSGIVING NIGHT, Michael and his family went to Grandma Esther's house for pie. As the adults talked, he listened closely to the stories while moving around the living room searching the pictures, knickknacks, and other decorations for clues. *A house full of memories and not a single idea,* he thought. He returned home more discouraged than ever.

The next morning, Michael awoke to the sound of Christmas music. A soothing baritone version of "The Twelve Days of Christmas" wafted in from the kitchen. He lingered under the covers, listening. He couldn't imagine getting or giving any of those silly gifts. They seemed so over the top and insincere.

As the singer wrapped up the twelfth day, a sudden

thought grabbed hold of Michael. He remembered his mother's words: "The things that are important to her can't be bought in any store." Grandma Esther had a lifetime of memories—eighty-seven years' worth—displayed on shelves and tables, stashed away in books, and stored in her head. But the best way to enjoy memories is to relive them. They come to life all over again every time they're shared.

Excited, Michael jumped out of bed and went straight to his desk. Taking a piece of lined paper, he cut it into twelve equal strips. As he recalled the items he'd seen in Grandma Esther's home, he wrote out twelve questions, one on each strip. In his closet he found a small empty box and wrote *The Twelve Days of Memories* on the lid before placing the strips of paper inside.

I'd better start early, he thought, *in case I have to miss a day for some reason.*

And so, the next afternoon, he paid Grandma Esther a visit. As she had instructed all of the family to do, Michael opened the door a few inches and announced himself.

"I'm in the living room, Michael."

What luck, he thought. *The perfect room in the house to start.*

He made small talk for a few minutes, trying to act nonchalant, before posing his first memory question: "Grandma," he said, sizing up a photo of Grandpa Paul in his military uniform, "Grandpa sure looks important in this picture. When was it taken?"

"Oh, well, that was a long time ago," she said with chuckle. "We were stationed in Virginia. Newlyweds with no family around, we had to rely on each other for everything. But we were so in love." A look of longing filled her eyes. "Every Saturday night he'd put on his dress uniform, just like in that picture, and I'd wear my blue chiffon dress. We'd go into town to a club called the Summer Breeze and 'cut the rug,' as they used to say. The music then was nothing like the stuff you kids have today. We had real music—the big bands. Dorsey, Miller, Goodman—we loved them all. And when Grandpa and I hit the dance floor, heads would turn."

For the next hour, Michael listened, mesmerized by the joy he saw in his great-grandma's eyes. That night, he wrote down everything he could remember in a journal he'd bought with his leaf-raking money. When *The Twelve Days of Memories* were finished, he planned to give the journal to Grandma Esther as a Christmas present.

The next day, Grandma Esther had warm cookies waiting. As Michael sat at the dining room table enjoying the cookies and ice-cold milk, he popped the next memory question: "This table is in all the family pictures," he said, tapping it. "How long have you had it?"

Her eyes glistened as she told the story. "Everyone said I should get a new one after Grandpa Paul died. But I just couldn't. It'd be like throwing away a piece of my heart. You see, we never had a lot of money. After we got out of the army, your grandpa worked in a sawmill and cabinet shop managed by his good friend Norm Fields. Always looking for ways to save a penny, Grandpa asked Norm if he could use some of the scrap wood out back of the mill to build a table. A true craftsman, Paul built everything to last. Norm said it was the finest table he'd ever seen." She rubbed her fingers back and forth lovingly across the grain. "Patience and love went into everything your grandpa built, and this table has served our family for fifty years."

The next day, the subject was vacations. "The old car in this picture sure looks neat," Michael said as he thumbed through a photo album on Grandma Esther's coffee table. "Did you take it on any long trips?"

Grandma Esther grinned. "That's a genuine '49 Plymouth Special. Grandpa thought we should try to see as much of the world as possible—on a budget, of course. One summer, he took a week off from the mill and we drove across the country to California, headed for the beach. Driving through the Mojave Desert in the middle of the day during the hottest part of summer is no picnic, let me tell you," she said, wagging a finger. "That old Plymouth began to overheat, and Grandpa got the bright idea that he could draw some of the heat off the engine by running the heater. Whether it helped at all I have no idea but, somehow, we made it. On the way home, we drove through the desert at night," she said with a twinkle in her eyes and a wry laugh.

And so it went, the next day and the next, each one with more memories than the last. So far, Michael had filled more than two dozen pages of his journal. He'd loved watching Grandma Esther's eyes light up with each memory question, and he was bursting with anticipation as he hurried home from school on day twelve. Today, he'd ask the big one—the question he'd purposely saved for last.

When he got near Grandma Esther's house, he clamped on the brakes of his bike and skidded to a halt. He gasped at the sight of emergency vehicles out front with their lights flashing. Dropping his bike in the road right where he'd stopped, he ran toward the house. His mom met him at the door and gently guided him into the open garage.

"Mom, what's going on? Is Grandma Esther all right?" The anxiousness in his voice matched the fear in his eyes.

"I'm sure she's fine. And we will be, too, in time." She put a hand on his shoulder. "I'm sorry to have to tell you that your great-grandma returned home this afternoon."

Michael's chest tightened, and tears flowed from his eyes.

"It's always hardest on those who are left behind," his mother continued, "but I'm sure she's very happy now, and we should try to be happy for her."

"But today . . . today was the . . . the twelfth day," Michael managed to choke out. "The day I was going to . . . to ask her about . . . her faith in God."

"Your Grandma Esther didn't have to tell you about that, Michael," his mother said softly. "She lived it every day of her life."

Michael could only sniffle and nod.

"Oh, by the way, we found this letter on Grandma's night-stand addressed to you."

A look of surprise crossed his face. "A letter? For me?"

Michael took the letter and he and his mother sat down on the bumper of his grandma's car and read it together.

Dear Michael,

Because you're reading this, it means that I'm gone. Please don't be sad. I've lived a long, wonderful life.

Thank you for the special Christmas gift. I suppose you thought I didn't know what you were doing. I figured after the third visit that something was up. No twelve-year-old should be that anxious to spend so much time with his great-grandmother.

You are such a good listener. Few people have this ability. It's a gift from God. He does it perfectly. He'll listen as long as we want to talk. And He never replies until we're ready to listen.

Reliving those memories brought me such joy. It also made me realize just how much I miss your Grandpa Paul. I'm sure he'll be waiting for me. I wonder if he'll ask me to dance.

Much love and thanks for the most generous and perfect Christmas gift ever.

Grandma Esther

Michael looked up slowly at his mother and wiped away his tears. "You know, Mom, I thought I was giving this really special Christmas gift to Grandma Esther. But after a while, it started to feel like she was giving a gift to me."

Michael's mother looked at him knowingly and gave him a hug. "Merry Christmas, Michael."

They stood in reverent silence as they watched the emergency personnel drive away. Michael imagined Grandma

Esther's smile as Grandpa Paul took her into his arms and they began to dance.

REFLECTIONS

MICHAEL'S GIFT

I grew up in a small house with two bedrooms upstairs and two in the basement apartment where my grandmother lived. I slept in the spare bedroom in the basement and had ample opportunity to visit with Grandma. I could have given her the twelve days of memories many times over, but I wasted the chance. And on birthdays or Christmases, I usually took the easy route and gave her a small knickknack for her living room shelves, which were already overflowing with them.

I wish I had taken the time to capture her memories.

SILENT NIGHT

The blue bomb swerved to miss a pothole, bounced hard on a broken strut then screeched as it righted itself and continued on. The harsh winter had chunked up pavement all over town and Aspen Crane knew her balding tires wouldn't survive a plunge into too many more road ravines.

She brought her rattletrap to a sputtering halt in front of Crestwood Elementary School, where her son, Cody, attended third grade. The car backfired then idled with a sickly hum.

"Hey, that's the best it's done all week!" Cody declared.

Aspen laughed. "I guess we should be thankful for small favors." Putting a finger on the tip of his nose, she said, "YOU have a wonderful day."

A huge grin stretched across Cody's face. "Have the best day ever, Mom!" he said, before rushing off to greet his friends.

She never tired of hearing those words, though, he said them to her almost every day.

While watching him go, she shifted into drive, and the car vibrated for a few seconds then stalled. She counted to ten before giving the key a turn. The exhaust belched thick smoke as the car rumbled slowly forward. Finally, the vehicle gained enough momentum to roll on down the street. Aspen said a silent prayer that the beast would get her to the local grocery store where she worked. She was grateful spring had arrived because she and Cody might have to walk everywhere soon.

They didn't have much besides each other, but most of the time that felt like enough. A shotgun bride, Aspen had been left by her husband to raise Cody on her own before their son was even born. Scandalized by her teenage recklessness, her parents had cut off communication with her.

With no support from anyone, she and Cody were on their own.

For Aspen, her little man became the hub around which everything revolved. Everything she'd done for the past seven years was for him; and all the happiness she'd felt was because of him. With the energy of a power plant and a smile as bright as a sunrise, he gave her the will to get out of bed each morning. He was the glue that held her fragile life together.

Cody had a battery that seemed to never run down and Aspen tried to channel that energy into meaningful activities. He loved sports and was "the best little shortstop" his coach had ever seen. Aspen thought he looked so handsome and grown-up in his baseball uniform. The team was undefeated in city-wide little league after five weeks and they were expected to vie for the championship as they headed into summer.

But as school let out for the year, in the second week of June, the game of life threw the Cranes a curveball.

On the warm nights when Cody should have been snagging ground balls or running bases, he went to bed early, listless. A tired, achy feeling had grabbed hold of him and wouldn't let go, along with a fever, chills, soreness under his arms, and headaches.

At first, Aspen brushed it off as a temporary wrinkle—one of those things they'd quickly iron out. But after a week with no sign of improvement from Cody, she had to admit that he might need more than tender loving care and home remedies.

CODY LAY SPRAWLED across two chairs in the examination room as Aspen paced back and forth, waiting anxiously for the results of a second series of tests. Their family physician had sent them straight to a specialist after Cody's initial blood work. Though Aspen had been bracing herself for any outcome, when the specialist entered the room and confirmed the diagnosis, she broke down.

"Are you absolutely sure it's leukemia? Could the tests be wrong? They *have* to be *wrong*!" She buried her face in her hands and sobbed uncontrollably, collapsing into a chair beside Cody.

"Don't worry, Mom," Cody said weakly. "It's just a wrinkle."

But some wrinkles can be tough to smooth out.

Instead of going to ballgames and on picnics, Cody and Aspen spent too many summer days at the oncology clinic. And for all the pain and discomfort they caused, the treatments didn't help. After months of chemo, Cody's white blood cell count had actually risen. And by then he was so sick and had endured so much that he begged his mom to stop.

The doctors had tried everything they knew and he'd put up a terrific fight, but by the time other kids were shuffling to school on a carpet of colored leaves, Cody was gone.

Aspen's heart broke on the day her son left. Now she had no one and no hope for the future. She cursed God for taking her only source of happiness and for ignoring the hours and days she'd spent on her knees begging for her son's life. He was just a boy with so much ahead of him, so much promise. He deserved to live. The flames of faith that once burned inside of her were extinguished by a flood of soul-cankering despair and bitterness.

After Cody was laid to rest, Aspen withdrew from everyone and everything. She left the house only to go to work. When Thanksgiving rolled around, her heart was so swollen with grief she couldn't think of any reason to be thankful. Instead of collecting leaves in the park for a colorful autumn collage and feeding the ducks that had postponed flying south for the winter, as she and Cody had always done, she wrestled with two weeks' worth of laundry. A frozen turkey dinner while watching a holiday special on TV was the highlight of her day.

Her anxiety soared as Christmas neared. The time had always been so joyful for her and Cody and the thought of facing Christmas without her angel son seared her lonely heart like an iron. Since she wouldn't be helping Cody write his usual letter to Santa, she decided to make a list of reasons to go on without him. Somehow, she needed to find some light in all of the darkness that had engulfed her. But day after day, a blank sheet of paper hung on the refrigerator door.

A major storm hit three days before Christmas. Heavy snow snapped tree limbs like twigs and made driving treacherous. The blue bomb had permanently died weeks earlier, forcing Aspen to trudge everywhere on foot in the bitter cold. On her usual late-night trek home from work, stomping along nearly impassable roads and walkways, a car zoomed through a pothole, drenching her with frigid water. The shock took her breath away. She hunched over and hugged herself tightly to preserve any remaining heat. Every inch of her, from head to toe, burned as freezing wind turned the water into ice. With six blocks to go, she forced one shivering foot in front of the other until she somehow made it home.

Too dazed to comprehend much while slogging through the snow, Aspen didn't realize the effects of the wet and cold until she stepped inside her house and was greeted by silence. And not just the lonely emptiness left by Cody's passing, but a complete absence of sound. No screeching hinges, no footsteps on the creaky wooden floor, no tinkling of the house key as it dropped on the kitchen counter. She couldn't hear—anything.

Aspen gasped. Frantic, she clapped hard several times next to each ear. Nothing. In a burst of anger and frustration, she clinched her fists and glared upward. "Wasn't it enough that you took my son?" she screamed. Then she grabbed a plate from the sink and launched it across the room. It shattered against the wall, but she didn't hear that either.

Overcome by a deep exhaustion, she plodded into the bedroom, peeled off her wet clothes, and then crawled into bed and sobbed until she fell asleep.

The next morning, still trapped in her silent prison, she got up only long enough to draw her curtains before going back to bed.

By Christmas Eve, a thick depression had settled in. Hour after hour she lay in bed staring into space asking questions that had no answers: *Why? Why Cody? If God is so merciful and just, why did he take my innocent little boy? Why couldn't it have been me instead? And why take away my hearing after everything I've been through?*

At the height of her grief, she jerked her head up in surprise. Had she heard something? Cupping an ear, she listened intently. Could it be? It was faint at first, then grew louder and louder until it seemed to be right outside the house. Wrapping a blanket around her shoulders, Aspen opened her front door to find a group of carolers singing a sweet Christmas hymn. And she could actually hear them singing. Her tears flowed freely as the carolers sang "Silent Night."

When the group had finished, a boy about Cody's age walked up to Aspen, looked into her eyes, and said, "Have the best Christmas ever!"

She felt her breath catch as the boy's words penetrated her broken heart.

Her gaze returned to the other carolers and they wished

her a Merry Christmas, but she could only read their lips. Throughout the beautiful carol and the boy's sweet words her hearing had been perfect. Now, once again, all sound was gone.

The choir made its way to another home, but Aspen remained in her doorway, lost in thought. As she pondered the words of the carol she'd just heard, a realization came into focus. *"Holy infant so tender and mild."*

God understands, she thought. He knew better than anyone about children enduring pain, about a son dying. And he'd let her know that Cody was safe and back in his heavenly home. Gazing up at the star-filled sky, Aspen imagined Cody could see her and was happy she finally knew.

That night, for the first time in a very long time, Aspen slept in peace—heavenly peace. And on Christmas morning she awoke to another miracle: her hearing had returned. She was filled with a joy she hadn't felt in months.

Throwing open her curtains, she welcomed the day. Pearl-white snow glistened as the sun peered over the eastern mountain ridge. A car towing a young boy on a sled drove by, and though the sight made her feel sad, Aspen smiled with understanding. She'd always cherish those memories of past Christmases with Cody—the magic of it all, the pure delight. The sweet little boy who had blessed her life for seven years would live in her heart forever.

Suddenly, an impression came to her. She tried to push it away, but it persisted. As she considered this frightening yet wonderful idea, the most soothing feeling streamed over her like warm rain.

She rummaged through the hall closet for something she hadn't expected to need this Christmas: wrapping paper. Taking a framed photo of Cody—one of her favorites—she carefully dressed it in bright red paper and topped it with a gold bow.

Then, bundling up against the cold, Aspen said a silent

prayer before venturing out for a long trek across town. Now at peace with God, it was time to make peace with her parents.

REFLECTIONS

SILENT NIGHT

It seems that life has no shortage of refining experiences. At some point, we're all likely to be thrown into the crucible of adversity. Such was the case with my sister and her husband many years ago when they lost their six-month-old son. The loss of a child has to be the most devastating experience a parent can endure. I'll never forget their heartbreak and the impact of that tragedy on our entire family. I'll also never forget how their support for each other and their unwavering faith in God carried them through.

If you guessed that the story's title is a reference to the Holy Infant and the reason for the season, you'd be mostly right, but there's a little more to it. Three of my four daughters and I have serious hearing loss. Because we take our hearing aids out at bedtime, every night is a silent night for us.

A CHRISTMAS PRAYER

Scuzzy Hackett squirmed on the threadbare sofa, trying to get comfortable. Leaning up, he put another fold in the burlap sack that separated him from some springs poking through the fabric. His sister, eight-year-old Emma, lay at the opposite end of the sofa, her head pointing in the other direction. Two tattered blankets covered her; their mother's coat was draped over him. Scuzzy burrowed his stocking feet under Emma's blankets since the coat only reached so far.

The last few coals in the fireplace glowed a dull orange. Soon the house would be cold, but he and Emma couldn't afford to be careless with their scant supply of fuel. Not with a long winter ahead.

With no curtains or blinds to keep its light from getting in, the moon beamed brightly through the back window. Sound asleep, Emma appeared angel-like as the light reflecting off her snarled strawberry-blonde hair made a halo around her head. *Same color as Mom's,* Scuzzy thought, as he gazed across the backyard of their lonely rural home to the rough wooden cross sticking up by the fence.

Only eleven, Scuzzy had buried their mother two weeks earlier, just a week before Thanksgiving. Using a broken shovel with half a handle, he picked and jabbed at the crusted earth, struggling to free rocks the size of softballs while Emma watched from the back steps, sobbing the entire time.

"No use cryin'," Scuzzy told her. "She's gone. We hafta find a way to make it on our own."

"Can't somebody help us?" Emma pleaded.

"Ya see anybody?" he barked, looking around for affect. "Nobody wants us. We don't have family or friends. The school doesn't care when we don't show up. We're on our own!" he told her emphatically. "If folks find out she's gone, they'll take us away. Separate us. Is that what ya want?"

"No, Daniel . . ." Emma said, her shoulders drooping.

She always called him by his given name. Scuzzy was a nickname he'd picked up in town from the school roughnecks—older boys who let him know that his ragged, grimy clothes and scraggly looks put him on par with animals. The name had stuck and most kids called him that—even some grown-ups.

Scuzzy watched a cockroach scurry across the bare wooden floor and through a tiny hole in the wall. *Probably goin' out for somethin' to eat,* he thought. *Sure won't find much in here.*

He looked at his sister closely one more time to make sure she was breathing, a ritual he'd begun after his mother had passed away during the night. He relaxed when he saw her chest rise and fall. Then, after setting his internal alarm for four o'clock in the morning, he turned on his side and quickly fell asleep.

As the moon shifted westward in the early morning sky, Scuzzy's eyes popped wide open. He didn't know how it worked, but he always woke up within minutes of the time he'd set in his head the night before. After quietly inching his way off the couch, he pulled on his shoes then slipped out the front door, leaving Emma sleeping.

After walking two miles on a back road and taking a shortcut through Cooper's cornfield, he stood in back of Denton's Market. If he timed things just right, he could usually snag the day-old baked goods right after they were pitched into the dumpster. Putting a foot on the dumpster's metal ridge, he pulled himself up and peered over the top. Suddenly a light flashed on and he jumped back, concealing himself behind a stack of pallets as the loading dock's overhead door lifted. Old man Denton himself came out to serve up Scuzzy and Emma's breakfast.

Elmer Denton was said to be the meanest man in town, always chasing kids out of his store. Scuzzy had never had a run-in with the old man because he never had cause to go inside the store without his mom. And now that she was gone, Scuzzy did all his shopping out back.

Denton tossed a sack into the big metal bin then went back inside. Scuzzy hurriedly leaned over the rim and snatched up the day's feast. He raced toward the cornfield with his treasure, unaware of the lone figure standing in the shadows, watching him go.

Scuzzy and Emma hit the jackpot that day: three glazed donuts, an apple fritter, and cinnamon bread. They ate more than they should have but still had enough for dinner that night. Lunch was a rarity, except for those days when Emma couldn't wait and Scuzzy gave up part of his dinner to keep her stomach from growling.

The next morning, Scuzzy arrived at Denton's to find a surprise. A plastic grocery sack hung from a bolt on the outside of the bin. It contained fresh bread (not the usual day-old bread), peanut butter, and raspberry jelly. He looked around suspiciously, hoping he wasn't being set up like a thief. But seeing no one, he turned and made a beeline for the field.

Emma couldn't believe it. She hugged Scuzzy so tight it almost took his breath away. They ate slowly, savoring every bite. Nothing had ever tasted so good. "Ya think God had somethin' to do with it?" Emma asked as she chewed.

Scuzzy raised his eyebrows. "Where'd ya get an idea like that?"

"Mommy said God watches over everybody and helps those in need."

"You can believe what ya want," he said, "but I don't think God gives me much thought."

As the weeks passed and Christmas drew near, Scuzzy found more surprises, and not just in the form of food. Curiously, they came in threes: three fleece blankets; three pairs of gloves; three sweatshirts; three pairs of socks. And one of the items in each group of three was always larger than the other two.

"It just has to be God," Emma declared one morning. "I bet Mommy told him about us."

Scuzzy looked up from his breakfast into the eyes of his trusting sister. He'd never had reason to believe in much. Their father had left before Emma was born. Their mother had worked odd jobs and barely made ends meet. He couldn't deny that it sure was strange, though, all this stuff appearing out of nowhere.

Emma's words weighed on Scuzzy's mind all that day and into the night. Wrapped in the new fleece blanket and wearing the new gloves and socks, he was much warmer than he'd expected to be at this time of year. But why would God give them all these things when he'd taken away the most important thing of all?

SCUZZY AWOKE on the day of Christmas Eve to find that a light snow had fallen during the night, leaving the landscape blanketed with white dust. It glistened in the glow of the streetlamps as he made his way into town and down the alley behind Denton's Market.

A little behind schedule, the anonymous giver heard the approaching footsteps and quickly hid behind the dumpster.

Scuzzy grabbed the sack hanging from the bin and was about to leave when he felt the urge to stop. Glancing around to make sure he was alone, he cleared his throat, bowed his head, and said in a soft voice, "I haven't been much for prayin', Lord. But it being Christmas and all, it seems like a good time. I figured I'd talk to ya here, since this is where ya remember about Emma and me. I want ya to know I'm grateful for what ya give us each day, especially for Emma's sake. But if ya care about us so much, why'd ya hafta take our mom?"

Suddenly overcome with emotion, Scuzzy threw the sack over his shoulder and hurried off.

THE CHRISTMAS EVE sack was heavier than usual, and it held more than enough food for two days. There was also a baseball, a small doll, and a bag of hardtack candy. He hid these things outside under a bucket, so he could play Santa Claus for Emma.

Scuzzy went back to sleep on Christmas morning after placing the Santa gifts by the fireplace. Exhaustion from weeks of early rising had caught up with him, and he was still asleep at eight o'clock when a gentle rap at their front door woke him. Emma was already up and playing with the doll, the juice of the candy dripping from the corners of her mouth. She sprang to the door before Scuzzy could catch her and pull her back.

Before the man standing on their porch could introduce himself, Emma turned to her brother. "Daniel, he sorta looks like you."

Scuzzy narrowed his eyes. He didn't spend much time in front of a mirror, but he could definitely see the resemblance. "Who are you, mister, and what do ya want?"

The man's eyes filled with tears as he dropped to his knees in front of Emma. "You're as beautiful as your mother."

Scuzzy's eyes narrowed. He watched the man with distrust. "Ya haven't stated your business, Mister. Why've ya come?" he asked suspiciously.

The man looked directly at him and Scuzzy saw kindness in his eyes. "I know that your mom's gone and it's time for me to take the responsibility I gave up more than eight years ago. I hope you kids will forgive me and let me make up for lost time."

"Are you our daddy?" asked Emma, her eyes widening.

"That's right, Emma, I'm John Hackett. And I want to be with you full time . . . if you'll have me."

Scuzzy couldn't shake his resentment for this man abandoning them. "If ya want to be with us so much, why'd ya leave in the first place?" Scuzzy said bitterly. "Mom had an awful time. I was almost glad for her when she died."

"There's no excuse for what I did, Daniel. I was young and foolish. But if you'll give me the chance, I want to make it up to you—all three of you."

"So, why'd ya come wanderin' back all of a sudden?" Scuzzy couldn't keep the hurt from his voice, which cracked as he spoke.

"Late one night, about a week before Thanksgiving, I was getting ready for bed when I heard a voice. Someone whispered in my ear that you needed me."

A look of wonder filled Scuzzy's eyes. "The week before Thanksgiving? That's right when she died."

"That now makes sense," said John, nodding. "The voice I heard sounded just like your mother's. But I didn't know she was gone until yesterday. The prompting was so strong that I packed a few things and came to town the very next day. I got a job at Denton's Market then watched and waited for the right time to see you."

Despite his anger and hurt, Scuzzy felt his heart begin to soften. Their father had been the secret giver all along.

"See, Daniel, I *was* right," said Emma, as she threw her arms around her father's neck. "Mommy did tell God about us. She was the angel who brought Daddy back home."

John scooped her up in one arm and wrapped the other around Scuzzy's shoulders. "Come on, kids, let's celebrate Christmas together."

Scuzzy looked out the back window and across the yard,

to where their mother lay. Suddenly, peace washed over him. He knew she was proud of what he'd done to take care of Emma.

And a thought flickered through his mind. From now on, he'd just be Daniel.

REFLECTIONS

A CHRISTMAS PRAYER

There are so many underprivileged and neglected children in the world and it's a tragedy. As a youngster, I was too consumed with things in my own little bubble to notice those around me. I mean, to really see them. I didn't understand at the time that a girl in my first-grade class was surely one of those kids. Our teacher would lovingly take her aside, comb her hair, and clip a barrette on the side to keep it out of her eyes. Some teachers are like that. Heroes. There aren't enough of them to go around.

That memory, and a few others, gave birth to this story.

What if a child is suddenly alone? What if they don't have a hero in their life—someone who recognizes their potential and helps them succeed? Someone who makes them feel important and loved? Someone who treats them as the child of God they are?

Remember the children.

FOLLOW ME

The Novelty shop was dark except for a dim light near the checkout counter. Several items were laid out in orderly rows across the worn Formica top: Band-Aids, ointment, gauze, aspirin; energy bars, nuts, saltwater taffy, bottled water; a flashlight, two plastic ponchos, an emergency blanket, knit gloves, and an envelope filled with cash.

A silhouetted figure hunched over the counter, carefully inserting the items into the compartments of a backpack. Abel Wiggins never knew what he might need. It was best to be prepared.

He paused when he heard the familiar mewing. He cocked his head toward the entrance to see the scruffy old cat he called Cratchit pawing at the front door.

"That time already, old friend?" He pulled out his pocket watch. The inscription inside always made him pause: *Forever Yours, Christmas 2009.* His heart ached with longing for his sweetheart. Abel stared at the engraving for several seconds, until a scratching sound brought him back to reality. Walking to the door, he opened it just wide enough for the cat to scamper in.

Cratchit mewed several times, as though dispensing vital information. As the storekeeper donned his coat, the cat paced back and forth. Looking repeatedly over his shoulder, Cratchit almost seemed to be beckoning the man to follow.

Abel flung a scarf around his neck, pulled a knit cap over his ears, and hoisted the heavy pack onto his shoulders. After locking the shop, he followed Cratchit into the cold December night.

Abel Wiggins was a changed man, though a tinge of bitterness remained in his heart. Twelve years earlier, on Christmas Eve, a careless driver had taken the life of his sweet Alice as she crossed an intersection in town. With her last-minute treasure still clutched in her hand, she couldn't hang on long enough for Abel to get there in time to say goodbye.

The townsfolk said Abel also died that day. Bitterness quickly consumed him and he swore to make the man pay for his mistake. Abel pressed charges and filed a lawsuit. The driver of the car, Willie Birch, served two years in prison, lost his family, and as far as Abel knew, was left destitute.

"He got what he deserved," Abel had said to himself often in those early years, but somehow it didn't help.

Christmas Eve the following year, the anniversary of Abel's greatest heartache, a ragged cat pawed at his door. The continuous mewing and scratching annoyed Abel so much he finally got up to shoo the cat away.

"Go on, get!" he commanded as he opened the door. But the cat acted strangely, pacing up the sidewalk a few feet then back to the door, over and over again, mewing and looking up at Abel as though he wanted him to follow.

"Blasted fur ball! Probably have fifty feline friends in some alley looking for a handout. I don't have time," he said as he pulled the watch from his pocket. The inscription caught his eye.

Then Abel once again looked down at the shabby excuse for a cat who seemed more anxious than ever for him to follow. "All right, for Alice," he said, remembering her love of cats.

The cat led him two blocks south and through an alley to the edge of town where a service road ran along an embankment that shielded a large canal from motorists' view. The cat ran up the embankment, back to Abel, then up to the top again and waited.

Abel made his way up the snowy slope, cussing the cat all the way. As he crested the slight knoll, he gasped at the sight before him. A car was visible in the dim moonlight with its nose fully submerged in the canal's icy waters.

The driver was attempting to climb out the front window. Blood trickled down his face and his left arm dangled limply by his side. A panicked woman and children spied Abel through the rear window and began pleading for help.

Abel called 911 on his cell phone then yelled at the frantic passengers that he'd flag down additional help. Within minutes, reinforcements arrived and a tragedy was averted.

That was year one. And every year after that, the cat showed up to alert him to someone in need: a stranded motorist, a woman with no food for her three small children, a family without heat in their home.

As the years passed, Abel's disposition brightened and he began to think of himself as a reformed Mr. Scrooge. It had seemed fitting, therefore, to name the old cat Cratchit.

Mysteriously, Cratchit showed up only on Christmas Eve. Abel wondered where the raggedy cat went the other 364 days of the year, as there was never any sign of him.

And now, here he was again for the twelfth time.

They trudged through the darkness eight blocks, then ten, and finally a dozen. This was the farthest from the shop that Cratchit had ever led him.

Abel recognized the location as one of the poorest areas of town. The cat turned and scurried down a narrow alley. Few doors and no windows could be seen in the dark, cavernous space, and Abel began to feel uneasy. But Cratchit pressed on, past foul-smelling garbage cans and stacks of boxes and pallets. Suddenly the cat stopped. Abel could see a man's bare feet sticking out of a large refrigerator box turned on its side.

Abel knelt by the box and called to the man inside. "Sir, I've come to help." After a few seconds he tried again, but there was no response.

"This one might take every ounce of strength I can muster," he said to himself. Grunting and gasping, Abel tugged on the man's legs and finally dragged him out of the box.

"No!" Abel cried when he saw the man's face. "Why, Cratchit? Why this?" He turned to chasten the cat, but Cratchit was gone. And there in front of him was the man he'd tried for twelve years to forget—Willie Birch.

Abel shuddered. Seeing the man in this broken state, from his hatless head to his shoeless feet and poorly clothed in between, the bitterness he had once felt was now replaced by shame.

Snow had begun to fall and it quickly covered the alley with a blanket of white. Abel felt a hand on his shoulder. Startled, he looked up, but there was no one there. *Alice,* he thought, *she'd want this.*

Though unresponsive, Willie was breathing. The cold had slowed his pulse rate considerably and Abel knew he had to work fast. He tugged the seemingly lifeless figure into a sitting position against the alley's brick wall. Slipping his hands under Willie's legs, he hefted the man's dead weight higher. Then, with a grunt and a mighty heave, he jerked him up and over his shoulder.

As Abel labored three blocks to the local shelter, his heart burned with anguish. *How could I have been so heartless?* he thought. His legs were rubbery by the time he banged on the door. A large, young attendant came to his aid and helped get Willie inside and onto a bed. Together, they made him comfortable and covered him with a blanket.

"Can I trust you to give him some things when he wakes up?" Abel asked.

"I'm not here because these people are an easy mark, pal. Besides, what would I steal?"

"Sorry," Abel said, shaking his head. "I didn't mean anything by it. I'm going to leave this pack," he said, shrugging out of it, "and a few other things I think he can use."

Abel took off his coat, hat, and gloves and placed them at

the foot of the bed. He then slid the backpack underneath. What he did next shocked even him. Seeing Willie Birch barefooted and poorly clothed in that cold, dark alley, and knowing he was the cause of it, crushed Abel's heart like nothing had since Alice's passing. Sitting on the floor, he removed his shoes and socks, rolled up the socks neatly, and put one inside each shoe.

"You can't go out there without something on your feet!" said the attendant. "The snow's really piling up."

Abel acted as though he hadn't heard. He thanked the man for his service to humanity. "I wish I'd known as much about love and compassion when I was your age as you do. Some of us don't learn until it's almost too late."

The frigid air took Abel's breath away as he left the shelter. Snow was falling in sheets. His chest tightened and he shivered uncontrollably as he trudged back to his shop, fifteen city blocks away.

Abel was frozen top to bottom by the time he reached the front door of AA Novelty. His feet were blue and swollen. Every step was excruciating. Shaking violently, it was all he could do to make it to his office in the back of the store. He dropped onto a ratty couch, turned onto his side, and forced his knees up to his chest. His teeth chattered so fiercely he thought they'd break.

Suddenly he felt very tired. Unexpected warmth washed over him as light filled the room. Then he heard a voice—the sweetest, most comforting voice he could imagine—"Abel, follow me."

"Alice," he whispered. He heaved one last breath, closed his eyes, and was gone.

At Abel's funeral, the week after Christmas, stories of his kind deeds were shared by all who knew him. Even Willie Birch was there wearing a familiar coat and pair of shoes. And it was said around town that Abel Wiggins had received the rarest of all gifts—he had died and was born again all in the same life.

REFLECTIONS

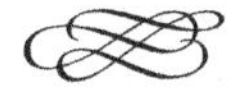

FOLLOW ME

There's no shortage of experiences in life that have the potential to make us bitter. Challenges abound. The cure for bitterness is charity—reaching out to others with love.

A favorite story of mine is *A Christmas Carol.* Though I've read it, listened to the audio book, or watched the movie every year at Christmastime for as long as I can remember, the story never gets old. I wanted to write a story that had at least one thing in common with this classic: a character who has a change of heart.

Though Abel eventually changes, it happens over many years. And the catalyst for change is charitable service rather than a vision of lost opportunities and the foretelling of an undesirable fate.

I'm guilty of carrying the burden of bitter feelings around for far too long. That kind of load always gets heavier as we go. It's never easy, but it's always better to remove the rocks of resentment from our packs and leave them by the wayside. We have enough to carry as we travel through life. There's no need to take along excess baggage.

CHRISTMAS FOR SANTA

Thanksgiving was less than a week away. Autumn hadn't yet surrendered to winter, though most of the trees had lost their summer bonnets. Red, copper, and yellow leaves tumbled across the playground. It would probably be one of the last days of outdoor recess for the year.

Seven-year-old Dane North hung by his knees from the monkey bars listening to his classmates Ross and Cade. He pretended to not be interested. Really, he just didn't know what to say.

"I've known for a long time," said Cade. "Saw my mom and dad puttin' stuff out on Christmas Eve. Watched the whole thing from the rails upstairs."

"Do they know?" asked Ross. "Did ya tell 'em?"

"Are you crazy? I'm not missin' out on any presents. If I tell 'em, who knows what'll happen?"

"What about you, Dane? How long have you known?" Cade gave Dane a hard push.

Losing his grip, Dane fell to the ground with a thud. "Geeez!" said Dane angrily, brushing sand out of his hair and off his jacket. "Why do you do stuff like that?"

"Keep ya on your toes," said Cade with a silly smirk.

"Well?" Ross said. "How long?"

"I dunno—a while. What difference does it make?"

Dane stomped off, still flicking sand from his hair and clothing. But it wasn't only the sand that was annoying him.

That night he tossed and turned thinking about what his friends had said. They seemed pretty certain, but Dane wasn't sure what to believe. Didn't Santa always come? Didn't he always eat the cookies and milk Dane left for him? Didn't Santa always bring at least one thing he asked for? And what about last year, when he hadn't told anyone but Santa about the bicycle he wanted? It had come anyway, hadn't it? Didn't that prove something?

As he lay there, Dane remembered his mom mentioning

that Santa was coming to the Brookside Mall the day after Thanksgiving. It would be packed that day for sure, but maybe there would be slow times during the next week when he could have a few minutes alone with Santa.

THE MONDAY AFTER THANKSGIVING, Dane rode his bike to the mall after school and stood in the line that was forming at Santa's Village. With only four kids ahead of him, he knew he'd picked a good time. And he was glad the gate was far enough from Santa's chair that the other kids wouldn't overhear him.

Santa finished with the first three children in short order. They were younger kids and their moms only wanted photos. The girl directly in front of Dane, though, was another story. Dane knew when she pulled a list out of her pocket that this might take a while. He tapped his foot and told himself to be patient.

As the girl on Santa's lap worked through her list, Dane started getting nervous. What exactly should he say? This year, he wouldn't be asking for toys. He just wanted to know —had to know—whether Santa Claus really exists.

He rolled his eyes as the girl continued pointing to the piece of paper. Suddenly, one of the elves stepped up and whispered something in Santa's ear. Santa's expression instantly went from jolly to grim. He lifted the girl off his lap and half ran, half hobbled toward the mall entrance.

Dane felt his jaw drop. He'd come this close, only to have his opportunity dash away. In a moment of desperation, he followed Santa as he raced out the door. He had to know where he was going.

Dane kept the red suit in his sights as he unchained his bike from the rack out front. Santa climbed into a rusted brown hatchback. Dane recognized the car but couldn't picture where he'd seen it.

Backing out wildly, Santa almost hit the car parked behind him. He zoomed to the parking lot's exit, stopped abruptly at the light, and almost hit another car when he pulled out too soon.

Dane stayed with him, though it was hard to keep up. He narrowly missed getting squashed by a dump truck when Santa left the main road and sped down a side street. He peddled furiously, determined not to lose sight of the brown car.

Santa made another turn and Dane, now tiring, started to fall behind. Frustrated and losing hope that he could ever catch up, he turned the corner and immediately clamped on his brakes, barely avoiding an ambulance parked on the street.

The emergency vehicle sat in front of a rundown frame house with peeling paint. Across the street, a policeman sat in his car filling out forms. And there in the driveway was the brown hatchback.

Leaning his bike against the faded picket fence surrounding the house, Dane watched and waited, though he wasn't exactly sure why. He wanted to know. *But know what?* he wondered. Surely this guy with the rusted car and rundown house didn't fly through the air on Christmas Eve delivering toys.

Somehow none of that seemed important now. Dane sensed that a dreadful sadness had gripped this house.

"Hey, you! Don't stand there gawking," an old woman called to him from the front porch of the house next door. "Can't you see what's happening? His wife's dead. Leave the poor man alone!"

Dane stayed put. Something was holding him there.

The front door of the old house flung open and a man in a uniform backed out leading a gurney. Another uniformed man followed. A white sheet covered whatever they were transporting.

The old woman's words rang out in Dane's mind: *"His wife's dead!"*

A hunched and solemn figure followed the gurney, still wearing the red suit but without the beard and pointed cap. Dane recognized the man's face instantly. He'd already decided the man from the mall wasn't really Santa Claus, but he hadn't been prepared for this. Stunned and feeling a little sick, he watched as tears streamed down the cheeks of their school crossing guard, Mr. Shivers.

Dane didn't know the man's real name. The kids called him Mr. Shivers because even in the most frigid weather, all he ever wore was a thin sweater. Rain or shine, though, he had always been there for the kids. And now he needed someone to be there for him.

As the men loaded the gurney into the ambulance, Dane inched toward them, wanting to help. But what could he do? He was just a kid, but he moved closer all the same.

The ambulance and police car pulled away together and Mr. Shivers was left to himself. He made no effort to move. His chest heaved as he stood there sobbing with his hands over his face.

Without thinking, just following his instincts, Dane came up beside the man, wrapped his small arms as far around him as possible, and hugged him tightly. "I love you, Mr. Shivers. I'm sorry that you hurt."

Mr. Shivers hugged him back. A minute later, Dane felt a tug at his shoulders. The old woman from next door pulled him away and shoved him toward his bike. Then she took Mr. Shivers by the arm and led him back inside.

Dazed, Dane stood by the fence for a few minutes, staring at the ramshackle house. After collecting himself, he climbed onto his bike and pedaled slowly toward home.

❄

He didn't tell his parents what had happened. He wasn't supposed to venture that far from home without permission. Even the mall was off-limits. His mother, though, noticed that he wasn't his usual talkative self.

"You were awfully quiet during dinner. Do you want to tell me what's on your mind?" his mother asked while he helped her with the dishes.

Dane dodged the question with one of his own. Maybe he could get an answer without divulging too much. "Mom, Santa Claus helps everybody, right?"

"He certainly is kind and generous."

"What if Santa needed help? Who would help *him*?"

"That's an interesting question. Do you have a particular reason for asking?"

He glanced away. "Just wondered."

She looked thoughtful. "Well, we recently talked about someone we can always count on for help. Do you remember?"

"You mean God?"

"That's right. Whenever we're in need, help is just a prayer away."

Dane perked up. He hadn't thought of that.

Once the dishes were done and he'd finished his homework, he kneeled with his parents beside his bed and said his usual prayers. But after the lights were out and his door was closed, Dane dropped to his knees again and said a prayer for Mr. Shivers.

As he prayed, an idea came to him like a flash. He figured that since people always wrote letters to Santa, he could send one to God on Santa's behalf. Maybe writing his prayer in a letter would give it more importance. Using a small flashlight that he kept near his bed, he found some stationery and a pencil in his nightstand. His message was simple:

Dear God,

I am writing the same as my prayer. My crossing guard Mr. Shivers wife died and he hurts real bad. He is alone now and needs a coat and some friends. My mom says you help everybody so please help him. He lives on Belmont.

Love,

Dane North

Dane stuffed the letter into an envelope and addressed it to God in Heaven.

The next morning on his way to school, he stood on tiptoes and slipped the letter into a neighborhood mailbox. As he rode his bike onto the school grounds, he noticed a new crossing guard. He was sad not to see Mr. Shivers, but felt better knowing that God would take care of things.

DANE'S LETTER made the rounds at the post office that morning. One of the workers recognized the nickname "Mr. Shivers." He told his colleagues that his daughter went to the same school and the crossing guard's real name was Morris Hatfield. A letter carrier who recognized that name described a home in disrepair and confirmed that the man could use some assistance.

That's all it took.

Excitement flooded the post office. Plans were made and assignments given. An army of the workers' friends and neighbors was mobilized. If young Dane North expected divine help, they'd give him a heaven-sized effort.

Within three days, enough groceries had been bought to last the entire winter. Crews were standing by to scrape and paint the outside of the house and clean the inside. And not one but three coats were purchased, along with hats, gloves, scarves, and boots for the man known as "Mr. Shivers." The children would surely have to find a new nickname for their crossing guard.

A GRAVESIDE SERVICE was held for Mrs. Hatfield. Only Morris and his pastor were in attendance. That's the way Mr. Hatfield wanted it. Small, simple, and quiet.

But while the pastor was speaking, the cemetery suddenly filled with cars and people. *There must be another service today,* Mr. Hatfield thought, groaning internally. How he wished to say goodbye to his sweetheart in peace. The closer the crowd came, the more frustrated he grew. Soon, though, his irritation turned to wonder and then amazement as men, women, and children approached to offer their condolences.

"We're sorry about your loss, Mr. Hatfield," said one man, shaking his hand.

A woman gave him a hug. "You'll always have friends," she assured him.

"You're welcome at our place anytime, Morris," said another, slipping a twenty-dollar bill into the pocket of Mr. Hatfield's sweater.

Then, with his parents close behind, a young boy threw his small arms around him and hugged him tightly. "I love you, Mr. Shivers. I'm sorry that you hurt."

Recognizing the voice, Morris looked down at Dane North and felt his eyes fill with tears. "It was *you*. That day at my house." He hugged Dane more tightly. "Your kindness got me through that first lonely night without my sweet Mary. I'll never forget it."

Dane looked up at him and said, matter-of-factly, "You won't be lonely anymore, Mr. Shivers. Now God knows where you live."

As Dane and Mr. Shivers stood there holding each other, Dane realized he no longer cared what Ross and Cade believed. He had his very own Santa Claus. And no matter what else he got for Christmas, he'd already received the best present ever.

REFLECTIONS

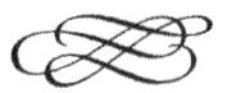

CHRISTMAS FOR SANTA

A wonderful man guarded the crosswalk at our neighborhood elementary school. For twenty-one years he protectively guided the students across a busy street onto and from the school grounds. Gentle and kind, he knew each of the kids' names and loved watching them grow.

Everyone called him Mr. Bus. The story goes that he had a horse named Bus when he was young and the nickname somehow became attached to him. All of the kids who attended the elementary school loved Mr. Bus. He was a fixture in their daily lives. We got used to seeing him, even after our kids stopped going to that school. Every weekday as we passed the school, rain or shine, he was there with a friendly smile and a wave for everyone who went by.

Sadly, we saw Mr. Bus five days a week, but we didn't really know him. Not closely, anyway. We just got used to him always being there—until one day he wasn't. He retired and a new crossing guard took his place. The new guard, however capable and friendly, seemed out of place. It's hard to fill the shoes of a beloved crosswalk veteran. We'll always be grateful for the wonderful man who carefully guided our kids across the street between those thick white lines.

Mr. Bus has long since passed away. When I think of Mr. Shivers, the crossing guard in "Christmas for Santa," I see Mr. Bus. I see someone special our kids will remember forever. Surely God knew where he lived.

Made in the USA
Las Vegas, NV
13 November 2021

34376510R00059